PIRATE STORIES

JOHN TOWNSEND

SCRIBO

SCRIBO

First published in Great Britain by Scribo MMXVIII
Scribo, an imprint of The Salariya Book Company
25 Marlborough Place, Brighton, BN1 1UB
www.salariya.com

ISBN 978-1-912233-51-9

The right of John Townsend to be identified as the author of this work has been
asserted in accordance with sections 77 and 78 of the Copyright, Designs
and Patents Act, 1988.

Book Design by Isobel Lundie

© The Salariya Book Company
MMXVIII

Text copyright © John Townsend

Printed and bound in China

www.salariya.com

Artwork Credits
Illustrations: Isobel Lundie

10
PIRATEY TALES TO SEND A SHIVER THROUGH YOUR BONES...

PIRATE STORIES

JOHN TOWNSEND

Stories that dabble in swashbuckling adventures at sea, hidden treasure, daring raids and scary villains have been told with relish ever since the first sailing ships set off into the unknown. Getting the shivers through storytelling has long been part of the seafaring tradition, and what could be more shivery than pirates, man-eating sharks and danger lurking in every salty shadow? After all, pirate tales can nudge us from our comfort zones, tingle our twitchy nerves and hook us into other worlds (yes, HOOK!) Either that or they'll scare your pants off. Hold on, me hearties...

KIDNAP

When Breon fell with a thud on the cabin floor in the middle of the night, he knew either his hammock strings had snapped or an intruder had tipped him from his slumbers. Unfortunately, it was the latter.

"Get up, ye sleepy bones... yer comin' ashore." The silver glint of a blade flashed in the darkness. Horror-struck, Breon blinked up at a candlelit scrawny face with sunken cheeks and hollow eyes – like a skull but with a matted grey beard flecked with festering fishbones. A cold, skeletal hand reeking of kippers covered Breon's mouth.

"Don't make a sound, young fella. Yer comin' with me."

Slowly the hand released its kippery grip as Breon gasped, "Who are you? What do you want?"

A bent finger wagged on scabby lips. "Sshh, don't breathe a word. I'm not 'ere to 'arm ye. You've nothing to fear if ye do as I say. There's someone what wants to see yer and it could be to your advantage, me lad. I've been told to row ye ashore in secret on account that it's a matter of life and death."

"But who are you?" Breon stammered.

"Ask no questions and you'll be told no lies. Just put it this way – your grandpa sent me."

"I haven't got a grandpa. I'm an orphan. You've got the wrong boy."

The man brought his nose right up to Breon's,

wheezing crabby breath laced with rum. "You're Breon O'Malley, right?"

Breon nodded, gulped and blinked all at once.

"Then you've got a grandpa still alive... for a little bit longer. Now, come with me."

The scraggy figure, with dagger clenched between rotting teeth, gripped Breon's shoulder and pulled him up to the main deck. They scurried in moonlight under shadows cast by masts and rigging, across the small sailing ship anchored in the harbour – Breon's home for the last six years. The air was still, the sea was silent, the night was warm.

Once down a rope ladder into a waiting rowing boat bobbing on rippling waves, the stranger pulled on the oars, and Breon stared helplessly as they slipped away with hardly a splash.

"Am I being kidnapped?" he dared to ask with a shiver.

"Not exactly", the man puffed, the knife now

at his side, "except ye have no choice but to come with me. I only get me pieces of silver when I've delivered yer so if yer try to escape I'll fillet yer gizzard from sheer annoyance. I've a short temper and I'm a dab hand with a blade. I can fillet a herring in two seconds and a boy in five. That's why they call me 'Bones'."

Breon thought the name was more likely from the sardine remains in his beard or the fact that he looked just like a skeleton with hairy ears and an earring.

"The captain and crew will wonder what's happened to me," Breon said as the silhouetted ship melted into the distance. "They've looked after me since my father was drowned at sea. I've been their cabin boy ever since. Please let me go."

"In time, me lad. Do yer do much smuggling on that there ship?"

"No! Captain Fleece is honest. He got his name

from all the wool we carry around the coast. That's our trade."

Bones chuckled wheezily. "I be glad to 'ear it. Now, get up there."

Mooring the boat at the harbour steps, Bones clambered out and led Breon up to a tethered black horse on the quayside. "Up yer get."

Breon scrambled up onto the horse's shoulders, with Bones gripping the reins before rattling up behind him onto a make-shift saddle. After a single 'giddy-up', the horse trotted up a cobbled street between fishermen's cottages, before breaking into a gallop on a muddy track snaking beneath the moon through a hillside forest.

Gripping tightly onto the horse's mane, Breon feared where they were heading and if he would ever return to his ship again. He was now sure the smelly ribs poking him in the back and the fishy beard prickling his neck belonged to an old pirate called Bony Bridges – also known as 'the Scurvy Scoundrel', notorious for surviving disease and death by the skin of his teeth – not that his skin looked healthy, or that he had many teeth. What few remained were likely to be shaken from his scurvied gums as they galloped on through the night.

Suddenly the horse reared, startled by a shape on the track just ahead. Bones pulled on the reins with a "Whoa there" and they slowed to a halt. The moonlight was bright enough for them to see a cloaked, masked figure on a white stallion. He waved a sword as he shouted, "Get down from that nag and prepare to be skewered."

"It's a highwayman," Breon gasped.

"I think not," Bones whispered. "Just do as he says and leave the rest to me."

"I've got no money," Breon said, as they both slid down from the horse.

The masked figure laughed. "You are the money, lad. I happen to know there's a good price on that head of yours. If they want you back alive, they'll have to pay up. You're coming with me." He pulled a pistol from his belt. "Bones and the horse are about to be slain right here, so stand clear, boy…"

As the assailant raised his gun to take aim, Bones seemed to transform into an athletic warrior with the grace of a gazelle. He ran and leapt at incredible speed, wielding his knife, which flashed in the moonlight as he struck. Breon had never seen such speed with a blade. Almost in an instant, the horse's reins and saddle straps were slashed. With a sharp karate kick, Bones struck the horse's rear as the pistol fired, missing him by miles. The stallion shrieked, reared and bolted, the rider tumbling disarmed off the back and crashing to the ground. Lying stunned on his back in the mud, the man could only groan as he squinted up at Bones, now holding aloft the sword and pistol, standing as the triumphant victor. With a foot on the masked man's throat and a flash of the sword, Bones sliced off the man's mask, revealing panic-stricken eyes and a scratched cheek.

"I should have known it was you, Sly-Dog Slouch. Ye failed as a pirate and yer've failed as a kidnapper. And what's more, yer'll be dead by morning if yer stay in these parts. Once I tell on yer, they'll be after ye. Anyone tryin' to snatch Captain O'Malley's grandson will be shark bait by high tide."

Bones whistled, his horse sauntered over and he nimbly mounted before scooping up Breon. "What's it like to be such a wanted little fella?" he laughed. "And what's more, I've now got a pistol and another sword to add to my collection." With a quick twitch of his heels, he shouted another warning to the still-winded Sly-Dog Slouch writhing in the mud, and their horse galloped on its way up a steep hill towards castle gates.

PIRATE STORIES

Although called a castle, it was nothing grand. No more than a fortified house on a hill with a turret for a lookout, it was a home for retired pirates of all ages. Guarded by those still able to shoot a pistol or wield a cutlass, this refuge had been bought from proceeds of piracy on the high seas. As few pirates made old bones (low life-expectancy being an occupational hazard), the castle had vacant rooms. One was occupied by a very old man, revered by all others: Captain Petroc O'Malley.

As soon as the horse clattered into a courtyard, faces appeared at an open doorway. A woman with a beaming smile hurried over, lifted Breon off the horse and shook him firmly by the hand. Others also rushed over saying "A pleasure to meet ye, Master O'Malley", until a girl appeared in striped shirt, headscarf and earring, looking every part a professional pirate.

"At last we've met! I'm Bryony O'Malley

– with a name and age similar to yours. They say we're second cousins a few times removed – that's because I'm always being removed for being too loud!" She cackled shrilly as she shook his hand. "Grandpa's been looking for you for months. Until recently he thought you'd been drowned with your parents. But someone overheard Captain Fleece mention your name and sing your praises so word soon got around that you're alive and kicking. Unfortunately, a few undesirables like Sly-Dog Slouch also got to hear. But when Grandpa sees you, he'll be over the moon. You'll do him the power of good and keep him going, as he's now very poorly."

"Give the lad a chance," Bones interrupted. "He's had enough scares for one night so best get him a bowl of broth and a glass of ale while I take the 'orse to the stable."

Late though it was, a meal of bread, soup and pies was spread on a kitchen table.

"This should make a change to fish and ship's biscuits," Bryony giggled. "Mind you, we have plenty of 'em here. Old pirates still want their familiar fare."

Breon couldn't hold back any longer. "But my father and Captain Fleece warned me about all the wicked ways of pirates. Pirates are 'vermin of the seas' because they're just greedy violent robbers. I've seen the horrible things they've done to ships they've plundered and left drifting on the open sea."

"Exactly, Cousin Breon. But we're different. It's time to give you a quick lesson about our wonderful Grandpa." She poured two glasses of milk and watched Breon eat hungrily.

"Yes, it's true that Grandpa ran a pirate ship for many years. Some of his crew live here now. But Grandpa was like Robin Hood. He robbed the rich to give to the poor. The rich were greedy pirates with their ships crammed full of stolen treasures and the poor were the widows and orphans of their innocent victims – ordinary sailors and fishermen lost at sea. So Grandpa became a hero to some and an enemy of many pirates, who are still seeking revenge. That's why this place is like a fortress. I've learnt to sword-fight, shoot and engage in unarmed combat. I can fight better than any boy – so watch it!"

Bones appeared at the door and beckoned to Breon. "Master Breon, yer Grandpa says he'd like to see yer now. He's a bit frail and not long for this earth but he's still got his wits."

He led Breon up a flight of stone steps and into a musty room lit by candles, with a four-poster bed in the middle. An old man in a striped nightshirt and nightcap sat in it, propped up by pillows. His eyes brightened when Breon entered the room and he beckoned with a bony finger. "Come here, my boy. Let me look at you."

Breon gingerly approached the bedside. "Don't

worry, Breon, I don't bite. And I ain't going to die just yet." He looked over to Bones at the door. "Thank you, Bones. Your silver is there on the chair. You did a good job of bringing the boy here safely. Now please close the door and let me talk with him privately."

Bones gave a nod, almost a bow, and left the room as Breon said softly, "I'm very pleased to meet you, Grandpa. I didn't even know I had a living relative so this is very special."

The old man wiped a tear. "And for me, my boy. You look just like your father. When he died, I was devastated and had no idea you'd survived. The last time I saw you, you were about three years old, nearly seven years ago. And now, at last, I am delighted to know I have two fine grandchildren who I might just persuade to carry on my work, should you so wish. And that work is to make our seas safer, to stop the evil pirates out there and to help the poor who struggle to survive around our shores. They tell me you're a good little sailor. Are you interested, Breon? Will you continue the O'Malley tradition – you and Bryony together?"

Breon held his Grandpa's hand. "I would love to, Grandpa – but how?"

"I have a fine team here – many of them are keen to get back to sea. They'll teach you the skills you'll need. I'd like you to be the next Captain O'Malley and run my new ship that's being built. She'll be a fine vessel and she'll be yours, if you so wish. You can name her and learn how to sail her. If you have as many adventures as I've had, you'll die a happy man, Breon. If you learn to read and write, you might well decide when you're my age to tell our stories and even write a book."

Breon knew his answer immediately. He'd always dreamed of having his own sailing ship. To carry on his Grandpa's work would be a great privilege. He'd already thought of a name for his new ship. As its job was to carry him and his crew across the sea, he'd name it just that: *The Carry Breon*. He felt it had a certain ring to it. As some of her crew would be ex-pirates, he came up with a snappy title for the book he would write about it one day: *Pirates of the Carry Breon*. He had no idea if it would ever catch on.

SHIVERS

THE GRISLY CRIMES OF CAPTAIN BARTELMY

When old legends of pirates and ghosts meet, you know you're in for a shiver of your timbers and a shiver of your innards - so keep a comfort–blanket handy, just in case...

There are villains... and then there are pirate villains without a single drop of human kindness.

The gruesome tale of Captain Bartelmy tells of

a manic murderer who, after killing his own wife and children, set sail to wreak havoc, fear and murder among sailors on the North American seas. Bartelmy gathered together a crew of equally despicable pirates, all set to attack and destroy anyone sailing the Atlantic coast and plunder any ship asail.

The Shivering Timbers pirate ship sliced through churning waves close to Canada's east coast. Any ship spied by the lookout in the crow's nest below a flapping skull and crossbones flag would be the next victim. Captain Bartelmy would shout the order, all weapons would be drawn and *The Shivering Timbers* would plough through the ocean to draw alongside and attack – with its swarm of killers sweeping aboard to execute the crew, steal the cargo and sink the ship.

"All in a day's work!" Bartelmy screeched with delight as the hold of *The Shivering*

SHIVERS

Timbers was crammed with yet more stolen chests brimming with riches. He commanded by fear, running a tight ship and demanding total obedience. Always impeccably dressed in black velvet waistcoat, breeches, frockcoat and knee-high leather buckled boots, his crimson tricorn hat was adorned with an exotic black feather. A studded satin and leather red sash worn diagonally across the front of his coat was tied around his waist, where a gold dagger and pistol were strapped. An ornate scabbard decorated with jewels held a silver rapier sword, often stained with blood. His crew, on the other hand, were shabbily clad in stained rags. They were no more than a bunch of scruffy ruffians, a pack of savage hyenas.

At the end of a windy October, when ships' sails were ripped to shreds, a battered *Shivering Timbers* approached Cape Forchu in Nova Scotia to shelter from the autumn storms. An eerie calm descended and, as grey clouds brushed a grey sea, Captain Bartelmy steered his ship packed with treasure: five hundred chests full of gold, jewels, goblets, silverware and weapons. He smiled smugly at the thought of such a massive fortune at his feet, knowing it was all his. After all, it was too good to share with such loathsome scoundrels as his crew.

By first light, a clinging sea mist rolled over the icy waves and the dark shadows of a rocky coastline began to disappear in a shroud of thickening fog. Bartelmy knew the tides here were strong and unpredictable but his newly gained wealth and power gave him added daring and swagger. Even the thundering waves smashing against a treacherous rocky ledge known as The Roaring Bull couldn't scare this fearless sailor. He was so used to being obeyed, he felt even the sea wouldn't dare spoil his plans. He was still revelling in his successes when the hull

SHIVERS

of *The Shivering Timbers* cracked against jagged rocks, split and immediately listed to starboard. *The Shivering Timbers* quickly became The Splintering Timbers as water gushed through the bilge and swamped below decks.

With churning sea all around and fog swirling the decks, Captain Bartelmy had only one plan – to save his treasure by hook or by crook. In fact, it would be by hook – Ben the Hook, his trusted mate – a plump pirate with a bald head, bushy red beard and a missing hand strapped with a glinting golden hook. He wasn't clever, but he was loyal. Together they would lead the rescue of the treasure chests from the flooded hold.

"I glimpsed a dark shape to starboard, Captain," Ben the Hook shouted in Bartelmy's ear, above the roar of waves pounding against the sinking hull. "The land's not far. If all the crew load the chests on the lifeboat, we'll get as many of them as we can to shore."

"We must fit ALL the chests into the boat. Every single one!" the captain bawled.

With all hands on deck, (as well as below deck and above deck) pulling and pushing at trunks dragged from below, each treasure chest was lowered one by one onto the boat bouncing alongside the stricken *Shivering Timbers*.

"The more we get ashore, the more you'll keep for yourselves," the captain told his men. They insisted on making several trips from the sinking ship to the deserted shore, where chests were soon piling up near the cliffs. After hours of fetching, carrying, rowing and heaving to make the treasure safe, the exhausted pirates sprawled on the beach. Bartelmy plied them with rum, told them to relax, unbuckle their weapons for him to look after, and to get some well-earned rest.

With a final creak and groan, the *Shivering Timbers* lurched for the last time and sank below the waves. The last chest was loaded onto the lifeboat and the final crewmen under the direction of Ben the Hook rowed to shore... where Captain Bartelmy was already plunging his sword into the backs of his men as they tried to clamber up the cliffs to escape. One by one they slumped onto the beach with bloodcurdling screams.

As soon as the lifeboat slid onto the sand with the last of the chests and remaining crew, Ben the Hook was already striking, before they could glimpse their friends' bodies scattered on the sand through the mist. With a few swift swipes of his hook, the captain's mate slit the throats of his remaining crewmen.

Captain Bartelmy patted Ben the Hook on the back with a hearty cheer as the last pirate dropped dead with a sickening squeal. The two men laughed at the pile of chests in front of them and the bodies of pirates strewn all around. Now the treasure was all theirs.

"How can we get our hoard to safety, Captain? We're miles from anywhere."

"That's my stroke of genius. All we do is stack the lot inside that cave in the cliff. We'll hide it with boulders, then come back for it when the weather's good and the coast is clear." Bartelmy's twisted grin belied his evil plan. After they had covered the cave entrance with rocks, Ben the Hook rolled the last boulder into place as Bartelmy raised his sword and plunged it into his back with a chilling snigger. "Now it's all mine!" the captain guffawed, as his mate fell dead at his feet.

By now the sea mist was closing in and darkness was descending. The evil pirate captain knew he had to leave this remote spot or starve. The rowing boat was no good to him now so he set off on foot along the shoreline in the hope of finding shelter or maybe a small town. The beach stretched on for miles before turning into soggy marsh, where he became knee-deep in tidal mudflats. His boots filled with freezing sludge, his usually immaculate coat and breeches were now muddied and blood-soaked, and his characteristic bravado drained into the clinging swamp. Cold and shivering, he slumped to his hands and knees.

Refusing to head back, Bartelmy struggled to his feet and plodded on along the water's edge. Exhausted, he could no longer move when his heavy boots stuck in quicksand and he was sucked down to his waist, as the tide turned and the waves lapped at his chest. He cried into the fog but there was no one to hear him. Only the gulls and seals heard his dying curses echoing around the cape as he sank to his neck and the waves rose higher. With a final splutter and salty gurgle, the pirate who'd cheerfully watched hundreds die at his hands now perished through the sea's timely revenge. Only his crimson tricorn hat with black feather was left floating on the rising tide.

Years later, during a stormy winter's night at Cape Forchu, the keeper of a local lighthouse saw a flare shoot into the angry clouds just above the Roaring Bull rocks. Assuming it was a ship in trouble, the lighthouse keeper called a lifeboat crew, who launched their boat into the raging waves and headed towards the perilous Roaring Bull. As they approached the hazy shape of a sailing ship listing in distress, they saw in a flash of another flare it was an ancient galleon with tattered sails and flying a pirate's flag. Its decks were piled high with treasure chests spilling over with gold. On deck at the helm, a

SHIVERS

solitary man in a black coat and red feathered hat grinned down at them, gesturing grandly with his cutlass. As the breakers overwhelmed their boat, the last thing the keeper and the rescuers heard was the spine-chilling laughter of Bartelmy's ghost before it was drowned by the roar of the sea.

Some say to this day that the ghost of Captain Bartelmy continues to haunt the Cape and the Roaring Bull, as he carries on searching for his hidden treasure. Any rescue crew summoned to save a vessel off the Roaring Bull rocks should be warned... just in case one of the cruellest pirates of all time is ready to strike again. Beware of a crimson hat with a single black feather!

ESCAPE FROM THE KRAKEN

Nothing prepared me for an unexpected adventure at sea when I was only ten years old.

Even though I grew up rowing little boats around the fishing harbour near our cottage, I'd never been far beyond the headland cliffs. These were the days of pirate ships sneaking into moonlit coves in the dead of night, smuggling ashore stolen lace, brandy, jewels or any other plundered treasures. But the ruthless bandits also crept in to pick up supplies and attack us. They came to kidnap strong young villagers, to drag them aboard ship under cover of darkness and whisk them away to serve as pirate slaves. My father always warned me to keep a harpoon beside my bed, just in case the press-gang pirates came in the night. "Lash out with that, Enyon my lad, and at least you'll stand a chance."

My older brother, Branok, had started work on the fishing boats and told me stories of the dreaded pirate ship *The Kraken*, seen sailing from the next bay early one morning.

"I saw it with my own eyes, sliding through the mist with its skull and crossbones atop the foremast. They'd been ashore to fetch supplies from the old chapel."

I knew of a secret tunnel from the beach through the cliffs to a disused chapel in the valley, where pirates were said to hoard their booty and trade it for rum or ammunition. It wasn't a place to loiter after dark.

A shiver ran through my bones at the crack of dawn one summer when my mother shrieked with horror. News reached us that Branok had been captured while repairing nets down at the boathouse. He had been bundled into a boat by a gang of marauding pirates and rowed out to *The Kraken* anchored in the bay. A witness said its fearsome Jolly Roger fluttered in the sea breeze, but its sails were not yet set and the tide had still to turn. If I was quick enough, I might be able to act before the ship disappeared beyond the horizon with Branok imprisoned inside. I had no idea what I was going to do, but I ran down to the deserted quay. All the houses were locked and shutters fastened. No one had dared confront the raiders in the bay about to set sail to who knew where? Wailing came from the bakery, where I learned that Morwen, the baker's daughter, had also been kidnapped – taken to serve as ship's cook. If I didn't try to rescue her and my brother, their fate was unthinkable. But whatever could I do?

I needed to see *The Kraken* for myself, so I ran up the cliff path to get a clear lookout over the bay. Sure enough, there it was at anchor – the only sign of life was a figure in the rigging and a rowing boat being lowered. Two men descended a rope ladder into the small dinghy to row ashore. This time they weren't heading towards the harbour to press-gang more victims, but towards the beach where the tunnel led from the foot of the cliffs through to the valley behind me. That's when the crazy idea hit me. If I was quick, I could get to the old chapel ahead of them. I ran down the hill to where the tunnel emerged beside the chapel wall. There were a couple of barrels still to be taken aboard. Grabbing a broken shovel from a pile of discarded flotsam, I prized off the lids to see what was inside. One barrel was full of what I assumed to be gunpowder and the other was some kind of alcohol. As that was easier to pour into the brook, I emptied the barrel, poked a small hole through the side, squatted inside and pulled down the lid on top of me. I had no idea what I was doing, particularly as the fumes made me lightheaded.

Before I had the chance to come up with a proper plan, the barrel shook and I heard gruff voices right beside me.

"Best roll 'em down the tunnel, I reckon. How about a swig of the rum first? I can smell it in the air."

"Capt'n Slash will give yer ten lashes even for thinking of opening it, and a slice through yer windpipe if you sip just a drop. Help me nail down the lid – looks a bit loose."

The banging above my head was followed by an almighty crack as the barrel was tipped on its side and I was hurtled around like a pebble in a can. Now my head was really spinning as the barrel rolled down the tunnel, as the pirates' cackles echoed all around. Next I heard the crunching of shingle as we descended the beach, then grunts as I was loaded onto the rowing boat. I sucked in the sea air through the hole I'd made then peered out to see a hideously scarred face with a matted ginger beard and a flash of gold earring. "This barrel don't seem right to me. It don't slosh like rum."

"Best not argue, Seth. The capt'n said bring the two what's put out for us so we're only doing as we're told. Maybe it's got a pickled mermaid in it!" Their guffaws were drowned by the sloshing of oars and the cries of gulls. I felt the boat beneath me swaying and rocking as we bounced through the waves.

"Looks like the tide's turning and there's a stiff breeze for getting us away fast. A bit too breezy to light my pipe."

"Not in here, you scallybog! That rum and gunpowder could blow us to the Caribbean and back. Heave-ho, we're drawin' alongside."

I felt myself being hauled upwards on a rope, swaying and clunking against the hull of *The Kraken*. Soon I was being lowered into the hold among the ship's stores. I saw nothing through the hole in the barrel now – just darkness inside and out.

I listened for any sound to tell me if it was safe for me to emerge. I heard the voices fade, the slam of a hatch closing, the creak of timbers and all was eerily still. I pushed up against the lid but it was rigid and the nails held firm. I threw myself against the side of the barrel, felt it rock one way then another... before falling on its side and rolling to a standstill. Now I could lay hunched up with my feet pressed against the lid. Kicking for all I was worth, my boots slammed into it with a crack of splintering wood.

SHIVERS

Eventually the lid split open and I could emerge – not exactly like a butterfly from a chrysalis, but as a rum-pickled boy petrified at what to do next.

The clatter of feet above my head, shouts of "All hands hoay", the clunking of the anchor rising and the tilt of the planks beneath my feet told me the sails were being hoisted. The whole ship groaned into life, lurching to one side as the rigging rasped, the sails flapped and filled, and we turned to head out to sea.

Thin cracks of light blinked from the hatch above me – over what looked like a swaying rope ladder. As my eyes grew accustomed to my dark, stuffy surroundings, I could smell a stifling mix of ship's biscuits, dried fish and lamp oil, with the unmistakable sound of scuttling rats around my feet. I crunched over cockroaches and stubbed my toe on a box of fishing tools, knocking over a cask of fishy lamp oil that glugged over the floor and a snaking rope. Fumbling in the dark, I touched the handle of a fillet knife, tucking it in my belt before clambering up the rope ladder towards the hatch. I slowly lifted the trapdoor – just enough for me to peep out at all the pirates' feet stomping the gundeck just in front of me – and the base of a wooden crutch. A chilling growl rang out, "Keep them prisoners bound tight to the mizzen and blindfolded till we leave sight of land."

"Aye aye, Capt'n."

Suddenly the hatch pulled up and a hairy hand grabbed my throat. It dragged me up and threw me, choking, on the deck. "What have we here – a scrawny little stowaway what needs putting out of his misery..." The warty-faced pirate in front of me, with bushy black eyebrows, savage eyes and half an ear missing, pointed his pistol at my head. I was dangling over the open hatch as he lifted his foot to kick me back into the hold. His finger squeezed the trigger and he wheezed with wicked delight. I grabbed his boot and clung on, the shot whistling past my chin and slamming into the hold below. Immediately sparks ignited the oily rope across the floor. The flame flared in the darkness as it grew and licked along the rope... snaking towards the barrel of gunpowder.

Whether it was the force of the firing pistol, me wrenching the pirate's boot, the roll of the ship or the shock at seeing flames erupt in the hold, the pirate lurched forward and fell through the hatch with a sickening squeal. He hit the ground far below with a thud, where the flames were now taking hold. I knew I had less than a minute to get off the ship before that barrel went up.

I remembered the mizzenmast was towards the stern of the ship, so I guessed where to head. I slithered away from the hatch, squinted around the gun deck and rolled into the shadows by the cannons. I lay very still until it was safe to run up to the main deck, where bright sunlight hurt my eyes and the risk of getting caught was now far greater.

A small rowing boat (probably the one I'd arrived in) was tied to the rails and partly covered with canvas. I darted over and threw myself inside, when I caught sight of a fearsome-looking man twice my size staggering down the deck towards me. He was swigging from a bottle, his head pointing up to the clouds, so I hoped he hadn't seen me.

"What was that?" he bellowed. "I saw a scrawny brat, I swear I did."

"With that rum in yer belly, there's no telling what you'll see, Ol' Jim. Just get on that poop deck and keep them eyes of yours peeled for rocks, sandbanks and hungry sea monsters."

As soon as the deck was clear, I untied the boat and darted from shadowy nook to darker cranny, with the salty wind stinging my eyes beneath the billowing sails. And there, right in front of me, tied to the foot of the mizzenmast, crouched my brother – his head and eyes covered by a hood, with ropes binding his wrists and ankles. He was motionless, apart from the gentle swaying of the ship. Just nearby, gagged, blindfolded and tied to the rigging, hung Morwen by her wrists. The gag couldn't stifle her sobs. Without another look back, I ran over and pulled away their blindfolds. "It's me, Enyon. We've got to jump over the side before this ship explodes."

With the fillet knife, I hacked at the ropes that were chewing into their wrists and ankles.

"But I can't swim," Morwen spluttered.

"I'll just have to teach you," Branok beamed. "Enyon, I can genuinely say I've never been so pleased to see you."

"No time to talk," I snapped. "Follow me..."

Suddenly, a shot blasted in my ear as a bullet

whizzed past my head and slammed into the mast in a flash of sparks and splinters. I turned to face the dreaded Captain Slash himself, waving a cutlass above his head with one arm, while wagging a crutch at me with the other. "No one boards *The Kraken* without my permission," he roared. "Whoever you are, you'll be shark bait afore noon."

As he lunged at me, slamming down his crutch to balance himself, Morwen threw herself at him, kicking away the crutch, delivering a swift punch and sending him sprawling. As he cursed and spat, I grabbed his pistol, Branok snatched his cutlass and we all ran towards the bow. By now other mean faces were appearing from all corners of the ship, to the sickening sound of daggers and pistols being drawn.

The three of us stood trembling beside the rowing boat, our backs to the rail and the coastline disappearing behind us. In front of us, against the gleaming white of the sails, we looked up at black billowing smoke.

"Don't shoot us," I shouted. "Please listen and you might be saved. You need to abandon ship. She's going up – look at the fire!"

A bulky pirate stripped to the waist stumbled forward and took aim with a bloodcurdling laugh. "That's the oldest trick in the book. We'd never fall for that 'look out behind you' hogwash."

A woman brandishing a sword ran from the poop deck. "Shiver me timbers, Jake – the boy's right – look!"

They all turned and cursed at the sight of angry flames shooting up from the hold.

In the instant mayhem, as pirates ran in all directions, the three of us lifted the rowing boat, hurled it over the side, then held hands before jumping into the sea. It was a long drop and the cold sea stung my eyes. Bobbing to the surface and gasping for air, we held Morwen and swam, as shots rang out behind us. We scrambled into the boat, keeping our heads down, and began rowing frantically to shore as fast as we could. By now *The Kraken* was engulfed in swirling smoke and before we had time to catch our breath, she erupted in a massive blinding flash and ear-splitting boom. Flames and debris flew high into the sky and rained down around us, fizzing and popping into the waves.

By the time we reached the beach and flopped exhausted onto the sand, *The Kraken* was little more than a charred, smouldering wreck in the distance, with just her bow and masts jutting above the water. The pirates and their beloved ship were going down fast, as Branok patted me on the back with a hearty, "You're one of the best brothers I've ever had."

Morwen laughed all the way home when I told her I was his only brother in the whole world.

If I told you that Branok and Morwen spent

SHIVERS

hours together because of their adventure, you'd probably think this is one of those 'happy-ever-after' soppy love stories. Well, although that hasn't happened just yet, they're now seeing so much of each other that I happen to think it's how things could turn out. Sometimes it takes a pirate or two to get my brother to take the plunge. To be honest, we could do with a good wedding round here. Any excuse to have a fun celebration and really push the boat out!

BLACKBEARD'S GOLD

Y ou never know what secrets might be hiding very close by... just waiting to be discovered.

A very old secret lay hidden in our family for exactly 300 years. Handed down from one generation to the next, an old dilapidated sea chest ended up in our garden shed... until I discovered a message from an ancestor. Or, at least, the mice uncovered it – just a few weeks ago. That's when I found out that the battered trunk once belonged to one of the most notorious pirates of all time. You've probably heard of him.

That mysterious ship's chest, with bits falling off it, had been gathering dust in my great uncle's barn for donkey's years. As children, my cousins and I played with it and even hid inside among the mould, cobwebs and rat droppings. Little did we know what else was concealed within. When Great Uncle Jethro died, we cleared out his barn and I was about to throw the remains of that chest on the bonfire. It was full of woodworm and falling apart, which wasn't surprising given its age: the date stamped under the lid was 1717.

Just as flames licked around the base with a hiss and crackle, I somehow sensed I had to rescue it. Something told me this old family heirloom, tatty though it was, needed to stay with us. Despite the churning smoke, I kicked it off the fire. Although it was scorched and smouldering, that old chest seemed to beg me to save it. That's how it ended up in my shed, with a pile of flowerpots on top. When the mice moved in, nibbling a hole through one corner, I glimpsed a secret panel with a folded message stuffed inside, written on old parchment. It told of the pirate whose name had sent shivers of fear through every ship sailing the high seas over 300 years ago. And, strange though it might seem, that note's special secret sent a shudder right though me, too – even after all those years.

Many tales have been told about the man who brought terror to the Atlantic Ocean during 1717–18. His name was Edward Teach but he was better known as Blackbeard. He was feared more than any other pirate when he captured a French ship in November 1717. After turning it into his own pirate ship called *Queen Anne's Revenge*, Blackbeard fixed 40 cannons on it and made it one of the most dreaded pirate ships ever. He fired thundering shots across the waves as the mast flapped his own pirates' flag for all to see. The flag showed a scary figure with an hourglass in one hand and a spear striking a heart in the other. That meant only one thing; your time was up!

Blackbeard was a towering monster of a man and he dressed to kill. Before he attacked a ship, he would dress all in black, strap pistols to his chest and wear a large black captain's hat. If that didn't look scary enough, he set light to slow-burning fuses and poked them in his long black hair and huge bushy beard. Just like little fireworks, the fuses fizzed, sputtered and coughed out smoke. Blackbeard, with his whole face sparking and smouldering, looked totally terrifying as he leapt aboard a ship, waving a sword and cutlass and roaring at the top of his voice. It's hardly surprising most sailors fled, jumped overboard or surrendered instantly.

More often than not, Blackbeard's victims gave up without a shot being fired, so he'd soon take over their ship, reward his men and keep the treasure for himself – locked away in his sea chests. One was the very chest in my shed where I found the hidden secret note. I carefully unfolded it and wondered what it was about to reveal.

The parchment was torn, nibbled, scorched and stained and the ink faded, but I slowly began to read the words written by my great Uncle Jethro's grandmother's great, great grandfather – a certain Elijah Farrow:

"We set sail from Hampton Docks, Virginia on 19 November 1718 under the command of Captain Maynard. He caught sight of Blackbeard's ship at Ocracoke Inlet off the coast of North Carolina on 22 Novembe. Most of Blackbeard's men were ashore so our captain gave the order to attack. We

outgunned and outnumbered the pirates 3 to 1. Blackbeard's ship had large cannons and, as we drew close, he steered into shallower water. Our heavier ship hit a sandbar and was soon stuck fast. Blackbeard manoeuvred his ship to fire a broadside so we immediately threw everything not essential to us overboard to lighten our ship and float it off the bank. This worked well, but not before Blackbeard fired more broadsides, killing and wounding many of our men. Captain Maynard ordered everyone below decks, while he stood alone at the helm to suggest he was the only survivor. This had the desired effect of making Blackbeard and some of his men board us. As soon as they came onboard, we all invaded the deck to ambush the brutal pirates. During the battle that followed, Blackbeard and Captain Maynard engaged in hand-to-hand combat. Both discharged pistols, Maynard shooting him at point-blank range, while Blackbeard's shot thankfully just missed our captain. They battled on for what seemed hours, Blackbeard suffering some five bullet wounds and many sword cuts, eventually breaking Maynard's sword. When I saw with horror that Blackbeard was about to slay our captain, I jumped on Blackbeard's back and inflicted a deep wound with my dagger. As the pirate fell, Captain Maynard grabbed my sword and with one blow severed Blackbeard's neck. His head rolled across the deck and I was ordered to grab it and tie it to the bowsprit of his ship, for all to see. When I threw his body overboard, some said they saw it swim away around his ship.

Captain Maynard commended me for my efforts and, on returning to the port of Hampton, he presented me with Blackbeard's chest, stamped with the initials of his real name: Edward Teach. This letter, together with the gold hidden within (a token of Captain Maynard's gratitude to me for

SHIVERS

saving his life), I preserve for my heirs with pride.

Midshipman Elijah Farrow, HMS Pearl,
1718."

By now, I was both amazed and puzzled. Was this letter from 300 years ago genuine, and what happened to Blackbeard's gold that had been 'hidden within'? Imagine my surprise when I poked a small screwdriver into the tiny space inside the chest where I'd found the message. As I prodded, something came loose and moved inside the little slot, but I couldn't see what it was and I couldn't prize it out. That meant tipping the chest upside down and giving it a sharp knock. A single grubby coin fell to the floor. How disappointing!

Was this all there was of Blackbeard's gold – one measly little coin that needed a good clean? But when I did clean it up, I was in for a real surprise. Not only did it shine beautifully, but it also had amazing markings on it.

I'll never forget the look on the woman's face at the antique valuation centre. She was a coin expert and said she'd never seen anything like this before – because it was one of only twenty such coins ever made. It was a very rare Queen Anne Vigo five-guinea piece, made from gold seized from Spanish treasure ships in Vigo Bay, Spain, in 1702. The last time one of these coins went to auction, it fetched £250,000. That's a shed-load of money – literally!

So now I've got a problem. Do I sell the coin and chest, give them to a museum or keep them in the family? What would you do? Of course, it's a nice problem to have – but who would have thought that pirates from 300 years ago would still be causing sleepless nights?

SHIVERS

For the record...

Captain Robert Maynard RN (1684 –1751) was a captain in the Royal Navy, First Lieutenant of *HMS Pearl*, most famous for defeating the infamous English pirate Blackbeard in battle near Ocracoke Inlet, North Carolina at the age of 34 years.

Robert Maynard's final resting place is in the churchyard of Great Mongeham in Kent, England. On the gravestone is written: "To the Memory of Capt. Robert MAYNARD a faithful and experienced Commander of the Royal Navy; who, after he had distinguished himself by many brave and gallant actions in the service of his King and Country retired to this place where he died 1 Jan. 1751 aged 67."

Maynard's defeat of Blackbeard is celebrated to this day. Every year, as close as possible to 22 November – the date when Blackbeard was killed – the crew of HMS Ranger commemorate the achievement with a dinner. The city of Hampton, Virginia, also joins in the celebrations by recreating the sea battle every year during the city's Blackbeard Festival, held in June.

THE MYSTERIOUS LEGEND OF OCEAN-BORN MARY

For over 200 years there have been stories of 'strange happenings' at a house in New Hampshire, USA. Rumours once told of pirates' treasure buried in the grounds and ever since, people with spades have tried to find it. Sometimes, it is said, they have dug up something else – ghosts from long ago. They say the shivers of ghostly pirates still linger...

PIRATE STORIES

The legend began in 1720 with a Spanish pirate called Don Pedro. He was feared by the many sailors who sailed between Spain and North America – a busy route for sailing ships, with rich pickings for vicious pirates. When *The Wolf*, a small sailing ship from Ireland, neared the coast of New England, the weary Irish passengers were thrilled to see land ahead – their new home, at last. Suddenly, their hopes were dashed when a ship drew alongside with pistol shots blazing, and a gang of Spanish pirates scrambled aboard. They yelled in Spanish that everyone would be killed and the ship set on fire. Robbing each passenger in turn, the dashing young pirate captain, Don Pedro, drew his sword to murder his terrified victims. At that moment, above their screams and sobs, just as his men began to raise their cutlasses and pistols, Don Pedro heard a baby cry from below deck. He ordered the ship's captain to bring the mother and baby to him immediately.

"Please don't harm them," Captain Wilson begged. "That little baby has only just been born." He dared not mention she was his own baby daughter.

"Do as I say," Don Pedro insisted, in perfect English.

The captain's wife, Elizabeth Wilson, was soon standing at his side on deck, a tiny baby in her arms. Don Pedro looked down into the baby's face and lowered his sword. He knew an old superstition warned that harming an infant at sea would bring him bad luck for the rest of his life. He turned and ordered one of his men back to the pirate ship, who soon returned with a box. Don Pedro took from it a beautiful roll of sea-green brocaded silk. He spoke softly, "If you name your daughter Mary, after my mother Maria, and accept this silk for her wedding dress, I will spare the lives of all aboard."

PIRATE STORIES

In the long silence, everyone held their breath. Elizabeth nodded silently, took the silk from him and Don Pedro departed with his men. As they sailed away, Captain Wilson and all aboard *The Wolf* breathed a sigh of relief, and they headed towards the safety of the harbour. From that day, the baby became known as 'Ocean-Born Mary'.

Mary grew up in New Hampshire and, in 1742, she married Thomas Wallace. Her wedding dress was, indeed, made from the sea-green silk that her mother had carefully stored for more than twenty years. The wedding guests were speechless at such a stunning dress and magnificent bride. Before long, Mary had children of her own but sadly, her husband died shortly after the birth of their fourth son.

At about the same time, Don Pedro retired from his violent life of piracy and wanted to settle down in the 'New World' to enjoy his ill-gained riches. Spending the gold he had plundered over the years, he bought a large plot of land in New Hampshire, where he had a mansion built on a hilltop. It was a spectacular property with tall chimneys and many grand fireplaces. Shortly after he moved in, Don Pedro heard that someone called Ocean-Born Mary lived in the same district. He remembered the baby from all those years ago and invited her to visit. Pedro was stunned by her beauty. When he asked her to describe her wedding dress, he had no doubt who she was. He asked her to come and live with him, promising the house would be hers if she would care for him in his old age. Somehow, she couldn't refuse.

Mary and her sons moved into the house. Don Pedro made sure she had all she needed, showering her with fine clothes and jewels, as well as a carriage and horses. Together they entertained guests at their elegant mansion and lived in comfort for many years.

PIRATE STORIES

Late one night, Don Pedro returned from the coast and Mary heard raised voices in the field behind the house. She looked out and saw Don Pedro and a stranger burying a large trunk in a hole beneath the trees. When she later asked Don Pedro about it, he refused to explain. "It was a private matter", he stated.

Soon afterwards, Mary returned home from town one afternoon to find no one to greet her. She discovered the servants huddled in a garden shed, too afraid to come out. It didn't take her long to find Don Pedro lying face-down nearby. A cutlass had been plunged into his back, pinning his body to the ground.

According to his wishes, Don Pedro was buried under the large hearthstone in the kitchen fireplace. Mary lived on at the house alone for many years until she died at the age of 94 in 1814. Ever since, people have reported strange happenings at the house and in the grounds.

SHIVERS

For many years, the house stood empty and dilapidated, with broken windows, crumbling chimneys and sagging steps. Local people sometimes saw lights in a window at midnight. Some heard strange cries echoing in the darkness or a horse-drawn coach pulling into the driveway. Those who dared to peer in through the windows claimed to see a woman descending the staircase... in a sea-green silk dress.

Then came the stories of Spanish voices drifting through the evening mist around the trees. Who was the mysterious figure with a cutlass – 'the fine-looking Spanish gentleman' searching with a spade beneath the tall oaks? Rumours and legends continue to be told but, as far as anyone knows, no one has found the pirates' buried treasure from 300 years ago. Not yet.

THE PEARL OF NEPTUNE

T he tropical island was surrounded by crystal clear water, coral reefs and shoals of fish in all colours of the rainbow. For the islanders, the warm white sands and palm trees may have seemed like paradise... apart from the pirates. Ships with ragged sails and the dreaded Jolly Roger would sometimes anchor close by to allow rum-soaked men to stagger ashore and steal whatever they wanted. They were always on the lookout for pearls. Rumours of a special pearl often brought unwanted visitors to the island.

It was known as The Pearl of Neptune, one of the largest pearls ever seen. Divers had glimpsed its shimmering beauty deep down on the seabed. A giant clam would open to reveal a dazzling silvery pearl inside, the size and shape of a coconut. Although far too big for any jewellery, it was an object of great desire – worth a fortune and a symbol of prestige.

Some said The Pearl of Neptune was made from the tears of mermaids weeping for lost sailors under the sea. But so far, it remained out of reach. Pearl divers had tried to cut it from its hinged shell, but those who did manage to swim so far down got trapped when it clamped shut. Like huge jaws locking on an arm or foot, the giant clam's heavy shell had gripped and drowned many a pearl hunter. The great prize remained unclaimed.

It was Sefina's idea to attempt a dive down to the pearl. "If the pirates know it's no longer there, they might leave our island alone. And if we could get the pearl for the island, our future might be much better."

Her younger brother agreed. Rangi was a good swimmer and had tried once before to reach the pearl but he hadn't been heavy or strong enough to get down to the seabed before his breath ran out.

He exclaimed, "I can now hold my breath for almost as long as a dolphin! We could paddle out in a canoe and take a heavy weight as well as an iron bar to prop open the clam's jaws."

Sefina knew the exact place to paddle the canoe. Although the sea was so clear, it was too deep to see so far down. Holding a net full of stones tied on a rope round his ankle, Rangi stood in the canoe and peered into the water below. With a knife strapped round his waist and clutching the iron bar, he was ready.

"Just a bit further," Sefina called, with a few more sweeps of her paddle. "Good luck, Rangi."

They were so absorbed in their dangerous mission that they didn't notice the ominous silhouette on the horizon.

Rangi took a deep breath, threw the bundle of stones over the side and jumped. The rope round his ankle dragged him down and down. He swirled through darting shoals of fish, past coral columns, swaying weed and purple anemones. When the stones hit the seabed in a cloud of sand, Rangi pushed the iron bar in front of him and dived towards the yawning clam with its giant pearl gleaming inside. He rammed the bar straight in and reached for his knife. With his lungs now gasping for air, he frantically tried to slice the pearl free. It was hard for him to see clearly now he'd disturbed swirls of sediment.

Clasping both hands firmly around the pearl, Rangi pulled at it so powerfully he knocked away the bar holding the mollusc open. The huge shell slammed shut in a spray of sand and grit, trapping his knife inside and clamping on the rope tied to his ankle. Weak from lack of oxygen, he struggled in vain to pull the rope or himself free. Without his knife, he couldn't cut his foot loose. Instead, he tugged at the knot but the water had tightened it and his fumbling fingers couldn't untie the rope. Bleached bones of other divers who'd suffered the same fate lay scattered around him.

Squeezing his fingers past the rope and into the clam, as the last bubbles spilled from his mouth, Rangi just managed to grab his knife from inside, slide it out and hack at the rope. His strength was draining away and he was drowning. At last the rope broke, he grabbed the pearl and kicked his way up towards the surface. The weight of the giant pearl was holding him down but he was determined not to let go now. He looked up to the light and the shadow of the canoe above him, and pushed with his last scrap of strength – up to precious air.

By the time Rangi's head broke the surface with a whoosh, huge gasps and coughs, he was convinced he'd never fill his lungs with fresh air again. He struggled to lift the pearl, which Sefina quickly took from him, as he grabbed the side of the canoe. Panting and spluttering, he was finally able to croak, "Maybe I'm not quite as good as a dolphin yet."

But Sefina wasn't smiling. She'd watched the silhouette on the horizon coming closer. The pirate ship was looming near.

Up in the crow's nest of the *Barbaric Buccaneer*, a telescope was fixed on two children in a canoe. "I think I've spied sommat int'restin', capt'n."

The captain was none other than the ruthless Scarmando Scarabzar. "What do you see?"

"I see two scrawny brats and somethin' gleamin' in the sun like a dirty great pearl."

Scarabzar's icy chuckle was enough to freeze the barnacles off his ship. "Then sharpen your blades, you seadogs. This'll be as easy as snatching candy from a baby."

As soon as Rangi clambered into the canoe, he and Sefina began paddling to shore. They didn't have time to admire the enormous silky pearl at their feet. Just behind them a rowing boat was already being lowered into the waves, with Scarabzar hurriedly climbing down to it.

"They're coming after us," Sefina shouted. "They know we've got the pearl. They'll kill us and take it for themselves. We'll never be able to hide it without getting caught."

"In that case I'll throw it back over the side. We can come back for it when it's safe. As soon as we reach the beach, we must split and run to the forest until they've gone."

He reached down, picked up the pearl in both hands and carefully lowered it over the side. He let go and watched it disappear under the canoe, sinking down into the deep blue sea.

"Just keep paddling and we'll..." he shuddered at the shadow passing under their canoe.

"What were you saying?" Sefina asked.

"I was about to say we could swim from here but we can't. There's a tiger shark right below us!"

Before they had the chance to reach shallower water, the pirate boat was racing towards them. With four pirates rowing large oars and Scarabzar shouting commands while waving his sword, their boat cut through the water at speed. It rammed into the canoe as hairy hands reached out, grabbed the two children and dragged them into the boat.

"Where's the pearl?" Scarabzar growled. Sefina frowned and Rangi shrugged.

"I don't care if you don't understand me, I want that pearl. We saw you with it. Where is it?"

Scarabzar raised his pistol and pointed it at Sefina, touching her chin with the muzzle. Maybe it was the lack of oxygen in Rangi's blood, or just a flash of madness, but he leapt up at the captain's outstretched arm and swung from it. The rest happened so fast that none of the swearing pirates had the chance to strike with their weapons. Scarabzar's finger pulled the trigger as his arm was pulled downwards. The gun fired, slamming a bullet through the bottom of the boat right by Sefina's foot. The boat rocked violently, men fell and Rangi grabbed Sefina's arm. "Jump!"

They both dived in the sea and splashed towards their canoe drifting close by. Scarabzar reloaded, raised his pistol and took aim. His men all pointed their pistols but the bobbing boat shook them in all directions. By the time the first shot hit Rangi's hand, the pirate's boat was tilting steeply. With all men leaning over on one side, as well as water gushing up through the bullet hole in the hull, the boat tipped up. As the next shots fired, it upturned, spilling everyone out before it completely capsized. The thrashing of arms and legs and blood from Rangi's grazed hand sent signals through the water. Far below, the tiger shark sensed prey.

Despite his injured hand, Rangi climbed into the canoe and was instantly paddling as fast as he could, kneeling behind Sefina, who was paddling even faster. They headed for shore, followed by angry pirates swimming towards them and shouting. Scarabzar, the strongest swimmer, was the first to catch up with the canoe. His hand reached from the water as he lunged at the side and held on. It was then that the shark rose from below and with a few sweeps of its tail, it rushed to the surface and clamped its jaws on his thrashing legs. Scarabzar screamed and let go his grip on the canoe as the shark dragged him under. As the canoe rocked violently, Rangi looked over the side to see an enormous shark diving to the seabed with the pirate firmly locked in its jaws. In an instant, the other pirates all turned and swam frantically back towards their ship, shrieking in horror.

By the time Sefina waded up the beach, dragging the canoe behind her, the first of the pirates was clambering back on board the *Barbaric Buccaneer*. He shouted down to the others, "Hurry – it's coming back. That shark is circling the ship!"

Gunshots echoed around the bay as pirates fired into the water at a fin slicing through the waves. The sea boiled and frothed as bullets peppered the surface until, suddenly, all fell still and silent. The sea sparkled, shimmering blue under a cloudless sky. The pirate ship's sails were hurriedly raised and filled, as the *Barbaric Buccaneer* turned to sail away from the island and out to sea... leaving its captain to his inevitable fate.

By sunrise the next morning, there was no sign of the *Barbaric Buccaneer* or its pirate crew anywhere to be seen. Sefina and Rangi sat on the beach beside their canoe and looked out on a calm and empty sea.

"One day, when my hand is better, I'll dive again and find that pearl," he sighed. "If only..." He used his knife to open the shellfish they'd been gathering for breakfast.

"Yeah, when there are no sharks around – just those dolphins like you," Sefina smiled, pointing out to sea where dolphins skimmed and leapt through the waves.

"Talking of sharks, look what's washed up at

the far end of the beach." Rangi was pointing at a large tiger shark lying dead on the sand. When they got close to it, they stared in awe at its massive size and broad striped back with bullet holes puncturing it.

"The pirates killed it after all," Rangi said.

"I wonder if it ate that scary captain," Sefina pondered, looking closely at the shark's teeth.

"We can soon find out," Rangi said, already cutting into the shark's underside. Sefina looked away in disgust as the revolting contents of the shark's stomach spilled across the beach.

"It's well known that tiger sharks eat anything and spend their time sucking up all sorts from the seabed but..." Even he had to look away as a human arm and a leather boot slid from the stomach with a splat. There was no doubt whose boot it was. It had stamped on Sefina's foot the day before – and the letters SS were embossed on the buckle. It was what squelched onto the beach next that made them both step back with a gasp. A familiar iron bar, a chunk of rope and something like a coconut rolled across the sand. But it wasn't a coconut, it was a silvery silky smooth gem – none other than the Pearl of Neptune itself.

LADY KILLIGREW'S TREASURE

Not everyone can say their auntie was a pirate. Mine was far more. Auntie Mary was a legend of the sixteenth century! Most people knew her as Lady Killigrew because she married a rich man called Sir John Killigrew, who owned a castle in Cornwall.

I was about ten years old when I discovered

that pirates came in many guises. Not all were uncivilised bandits who robbed ships on the high seas. Some were quite different. When I once went to stay with auntie Mary in her castle by the sea, I found out how many people living along the coast stole from passing ships carrying valuable cargo. I was stunned when my Auntie winked and whispered in my ear, "What better way to get rich quick than to pilfer from floating stores of treasure? After all, it's such fun. And I'll tell you a little secret, my dear. My father was a pirate many years ago, so piracy is in my blood." She gave a chuckle and another wink. "It can get rather boring stuck in this big old castle when your uncle is away on business. A bit of adventure along this coast can be so exciting — you never know what you're going to find next."

Of course, I knew about the rumours. Whenever storms swept in across the sea, some local villagers 'disappeared'. The harbour inns filled with normally respectable people, who gathered like sharks to plot their next attack. They sniffed the winds, sensed prey and turned into smugglers, wreckers and 'land pirates'. Their eyes fixed on ships just offshore – almost within touching distance. When the waves grew to such a terrifying size, so did temptation. Foundering ships became rich pickings. When the law made it illegal to claim salvage from a wrecked ship if anyone onboard was alive, you can imagine how sport turned to murder. On many a stormy night, lawless bandits were waiting to do the unthinkable. Auntie Mary was appalled.

"What is the world coming to?" she said to me at supper one night. "These murderous peasants are giving us decent pirates a bad name. They even light lamps on clifftops to confuse sailors, who are fooled into thinking that lighthouses are marking safe channels for them to sail through. Instead, ships are lured onto treacherous rocks.

SHIVERS

Then the gangs attack. It's dreadful – barbaric. No, my way is far more respectable and civilised."

"But you're still a thief, aren't you, Auntie Mary?"

She smiled. "Only if I get caught. Otherwise, I'm just a gambler. That's the thrill of it."

I looked out from her window across the stretch of sea where sailing ships were moving in and out of the harbour. "If you get caught, you'll be executed like that pirate on the quayside," I said, pointing to the gallows with an iron cage hanging from it. Inside that cage, the body of an executed pirate swung in the wind, being pecked by gulls. It was a warning to all pirates of what to expect if they were caught and it gave me the shivers whenever I saw it.

"Yes, that's poor Polly Marrak. She got careless when stealing lace from a French ship. I admit the noose is an occupational hazard but I have friends in high places who approve of my business. Come with me and I'll explain."

She held my hand and led me across the room to a large bookcase. She reached up to a leather-bound book with gold lettering on the spine. It was titled *British Privateers*.

"I get a mention in this book," she smiled. "That's because I wrote it. Of course, I don't use my real name. A privateer is simply an official pirate who works on behalf of the Queen."

She reached inside the shelf, pulled a catch and slid the bookcase to one side, to reveal a secret doorway with a dark passage beyond. Gripping my hand tightly, she led me through and lit a candle on a ledge just inside. Holding the dancing flame in front of her, she led the way down stone spiral steps, our footsteps echoing in the cold, flickering shadows.

Our steamy breath swirled in the candlelight as Auntie Mary held my arm and ushered me into a gloomy cellar. Around the walls, brass holders held candles covered in lumps of congealed wax, like icicles. Holding her candle to each wick, Auntie Mary began to light up the whole room. As each candle flickered into life, its mesmerising shimmer glinted in gold and silver goblets spilling from bronze chests encrusted with jewels. Trunks brimming with diamonds, rubies and emeralds winked in the dancing candlelight and, as the last candle began to burn brightly, the whole room was bathed in a magical glow of glinting, sparkling brilliance. I was completely bedazzled!

"Pretty, isn't it?" my auntie giggled. "It's all worth a fortune and Her Majesty is very grateful. It now belongs to her. Most of this treasure is Spanish and Portuguese. As those countries aren't too friendly with us at the moment, I simply see my work as a type of payback. After all, they've stolen enough from us over the years so I'm just helping them with their repayments.

Oh, I do love that diamond tiara over there. I may keep that one for myself. If there's a little jewel that catches your eye, just say so and you can have it for your birthday. That's if you help me with a little job I have to do this evening. Tonight I plan to rob a Spanish galleon just across the water. Interested?"

When we were back in the dining room, where a long polished table was set with fine china and silverware, my auntie pointed through the window to a ship anchored in the sound.

"There she is. She's called *Marie of San Sebastian* and she's packed to the gunnels with riches. She's awash with Spanish gold and silver. Later tonight I'll be boarding her with my team and bringing the lot back here to stock another cellar. It's terribly exciting."

I looked out at the magnificent ship in horror. "But Auntie Mary, it's got cannons. They'll blast you out of the water. They could strike this room from there."

She laughed. "That's why I'm a genius. Not a shot will be fired. And do you know why? The captain and his crew won't be there. The ship will only have a pair of tipsy cabin boys to guard her. It will be so easy and such fun."

"How can you be so sure?"

"Because I've invited the captain and crew here. I will be hosting them for a light supper before they move on to a full dinner and entertainment in the town. The duke and duchess, very good friends of mine, will wine and dine the Spaniards until I have stripped their entire ship. By the time they return to it in the early hours, my servants and I will have emptied the lot and rowed the glorious hoard back here in the moonlight. You can help us if you like. It will be an adventure to die for."

So that was my dilemma. Should I join Auntie Mary in her raiding party and take part in all that excitement on a clear, crisp January night at sea, or should I go home to bed and forget it? Should I become a pirate and plunder foreign riches, or hold firm to my principles of honesty and morality? What would you do? Would you choose risk, adventure and thievery or safety, security and respectability?

I chose to reject Auntie Mary's invitation to join her that night. You might think I was being dull and boring. But it turned out to be the right choice.

During the raid, a Spanish sailor on board the ship was killed in a fight. Although everything else went to plan, with all the treasure safely taken back to Mary's castle, she and several of her staff were later arrested. My uncle and I went to the trial, where we knew Auntie Mary would be sentenced to death. Had I chosen to join her that night, I would also have been facing public execution. There again, I should have remembered Auntie Mary was something of a legend in her own lifetime... and many legends have had happy endings...

For the record...

If you go to Falmouth in Cornwall today, you can see the places Mary Killigrew knew so well. You can also read the guidebooks about the famous 'Lady Pirate' of the 1580s:

"When it came time for her trial, Lady Mary Killigrew surprisingly received a full pardon from Queen Elizabeth I... but alas, her servants were not as lucky and were all executed. The Killigrew family business endured for centuries, as they continued to amass vast wealth through piracy, looting and wrecking in Cornwall."

GHOST SHIP

Back in the times of pirate ships,
A ghostly tale was told
Of eerie shadows in sea mist
And sunken pirates' gold.

A ship sailed from New Jersey's coast
Through squalling wind and rain
Packed with pirates' stolen gold,
Sailing home to Spain.

SHIVERS

The pirate captain, Don Sandovate
Steered through raging seas,
His ruthless pirate crew intent
To bring him to his knees.

They plotted mutiny aboard,
To take the gold and flee,
Leaving ship and captain dead
To drift across the sea.

Three days from Spanish shores they struck
And took control at last,
Attacked the captain on the deck
And tied him to the mast.

The pirates cheered, the sea fell calm,
The sun rose in the sky,
The heat beat down upon the deck,
The captain left to die.

PIRATE STORIES

He pleaded with his mutinous crew
To grant him just one sip,
As thirst burned in his rasping throat
Upon the scorching ship.

There was no breeze, the ship becalmed,
With neither breath nor motion.
In searing heat, Don Sandovate
Cried out across the ocean...

"Water, water, everywhere,
And all the timbers shrink;
Water, water, everywhere,
Nor any drop to drink."

His body, wracked with pain and thirst,
He screamed across the ship,
"I beg thee, bring me water here,
And give me just one sip."

SHIVERS

The pirates scoffed and held aloft
Fresh water, sweet and clear
And placed jugs cruelly out of reach,
So far and yet so near.

Each day and night, they took delight
In their relentless taunting
Until one night he breathed his last,
That final gasp so haunting...

Within an instant of his death,
A chilling windstorm blew,
So fierce it raged, the sails were torn,
And swelling breakers grew.

As lightning flashed, the pirate ship
Was tossed on seething seas
But with no captain at the helm,
Who had the expertise?

PIRATE STORIES

And so, the ship was thrown into
A trough below huge waves
That crashed and wrecked the smitten ship...
As men fell to their graves.

That pirate ship slipped far below,
To screams of all her crew
Drowned out by roars of pounding waves,
As still the tempest blew.

The ship was sunk and all men lost
Amidst that stormy blast...
The body of Don Sandevate
Still lashed up to the mast.

A legend tells the sea spits up
What it cannot hold...
After that pirate ship went down,
A shivery tale was told.

SHIVERS

An eerie ghost ship soon appeared
In the calm before a storm,
A Spanish treasure ship, no less,
In wrecked and ghostly form.

Its sails were torn, its rigging ripped,
Its poop deck overcast,
With a Spanish pirate captain's corpse
Still tethered to the mast.

They say, today, you might well glimpse,
Still drifting through the mist
A ghostly ship with skeleton crew,
The stories still persist...

The creaking ship, with ragged sails
And pirate flag a-quiver
Still haunts the seas, so sailors tell,
And casts an icy shiver.

PIRATE STORIES

It passes on its hellish way,
To vanish through the mists,
The pirate skeletons aboard
All wave their bony fists.

And still you'll hear the captain groan,
While tethered to his ship,
"I beg thee, bring me water here,
And give me just one sip."

Some nights his whisper fills the breeze
That blows along the coast...
His sighs tell all it's thirsty work
As a famous pirate ghost!

KEY TO A DEAD MAN'S CHEST

Petroc O'Malley lay propped up in bed, wheezing what he called his 'death rattle'.

"I haven't got long left, Breon," he told his grandson, "so sit close and listen. What I'm about to tell you will lead you to a hidden chest of riches that I want you and Bryony to use to help widows and orphans of the sea."

Breon beckoned his cousin to join him, as their grandpa took a sip of water and began to explain their task. "When I was a pirate captain, robbing the rich to help the poor, I had an arch enemy. He was the evillest pirate of them all

— Captain Dug Skullery. He and his vicious gang live on Sabretooth Island, which they guard day and night. Somewhere on that island is a chest of buried treasure worth a fortune, known as the Dead Man's Chest. Both of us were determined to find it, but neither of us knows exactly where it is. He's still searching but I have a scrap of paper that he needs to go with another scrap in his possession. When both scraps are put together, the clues will lead you to the treasure."

His shaky hand reached under his pillow where a small piece of parchment lay neatly pressed, with a torn edge. "I don't know what it means, but it's your job to fit it with Skullery's other half and to find that chest before he gets his wicked hands on it."

"So why have you only got half of the clues, Grandpa?" Bryony asked.

"Because Iron-Fist Frank, who buried the chest, kept the two parts of the secret message apart, on two different ships, to make sure they didn't fall into the wrong hands. Skullery made him walk the plank into shark-infested waters before Frank could tell him more. I managed to get my hands on one half of the message and Skullery got the other. They say he keeps his in a locket round his neck. But unless you get it and put the two bits together, they make no sense at all."

He carefully placed the scrap of parchment into Breon's hand. It said: *6S9 MN*.

Bryony stared at the letters and numbers with bewilderment. "That doesn't mean a thing!"

"I never said it would be easy," Grandpa wheezed. "If you succeed in finding that treasure, you'll not just thwart my old arch enemy, but you'll be able to carry on my work of funding the orphanage in town from those riches stolen by pirates long ago."

Breon didn't need time to answer. "It will be

my privilege to carry on your work, Grandpa."

He saw the relief in his grandpa's face. "You're a fine lad," he sighed, "but you must take great care. Skullery is a brutal murderer and his island is full of danger. You must take my ship and some of my old crew, including Bones. I know he looks mean, but he's loyal – there's no bones about it! His heart's in the right place. Let's just hope it keeps ticking."

Bones stood at the foot of the bed, with a broad grin. "It will be my pleasure, sir. Bony Bridges at your service, Master Breon and Miss Bryony. I might be old and bony, but I'm a dab hand with a cutlass and I happen to know that scoundrel Skullery. I can't wait to see his face when we steal back that hoard from under his nose."

"Just one more thing..." Petroc O'Malley continued, struggling to catch his breath. "Skullery's vile daughter-in-law rules the roost on Sabretooth Island. She's the craziest pirate of them all. They call her Birdie 'Crazy-Eyes' Raven and they say she eats her enemy's hearts fried in snake fat for her breakfast. I prefer a kipper and toast for mine." He gave a short chuckle before choking and wheezing loudly. "I must rest," he spluttered. "Come back and tell me you've succeeded and you'll give me a new lease of life. If I hear you've failed, that will finish me off. No pressure." He smiled, sank back into his pillows and closed his eyes.

"It looks like we've got a tough mission," Bryony said as soon as they left the bedroom. "We've got to sail across the ocean, outsmart a group of savage pirates, crack a coded message, search for treasure and bring it all back!"

"Not only that," Bones added, with a sinister smile. "Sabretooth Island is a jungle full of deadly snakes. And somewhere in the middle, on a smouldering volcano, is a pillar of rock called Blood Stone, where Skullery sacrifices all trespassers on his island, then strings them up for the vultures to finish off." He lowered his voice to the faintest whisper. "Your Grandpa doesn't know this but twice in the last year Skullery and Birdie have been here to get their hands on this half of the secret message. We managed to fight them off – but it's only a matter of time before they find a way to get that piece of paper you've got in your hands, so keep it safe, Master Breon. Now, while you get yourselves sorted, I'll be getting the ship and crew ready for our trip to Sabretooth Island. I reckon it could be quite a trip, too!"

A string of uninhabited islands appeared on the horizon. Bones steered the ship towards a rocky outcrop at one end, where smoke rose in wisps.

SHIVERS

"We can hide the ship behind that volcanic rock where the smoke hangs over the sea. It will keep us out of sight from Sabretooth Island. We can row over to it under cover of darkness. Skullery will have cannons pointing out to sea for anyone who dares approach in daylight."

By the time a new moon glinted on the midnight sea, a small rowing boat approached Sabretooth Island, surrounded by a smoky mist. Bones pulled on the oars as Bryony peered through a telescope at all the skull and crossbones painted on the rocks. Large signs in different languages said: KEEP OUT OR DIE.

"You can't beat a warm welcome," she whispered.

"If I remember rightly," Bones murmured, "Skullery sleeps in a cave near the beach just ahead. One of us needs to sneak in and get the locket from round his neck. Someone with a steady hand and nerves of steel."

"That's me," Bryony mouthed, without making a sound. "I'll do it."

Breon pulled the boat up the beach with only the faintest crunch of shingle. He hid it silently in a clump of ferns, dodging a snake slipping over the sand with a menacing hiss. As he turned, he gasped at two huge dogs bounding towards him, snarling and baring their teeth in a spray of steamy spit. Bones quickly reached in his bag and threw chunks of meat, which they caught mid-air and instantly gobbled up.

"I always carry bits of whale meat, just in case," winked Bones, "soaked in a special mixture from an apothecary friend of mine. It should work in about... ah, it already has."

Both dogs were already flopping on their sides, panting, drooling and stunned.

"Now we can approach the cave without being ripped apart," he whispered with a wink.

The cave bedroom looked surprisingly cosy. It

was just like a ship's cabin inside, having all the trappings of ships' brasses, compass, wheel, a sail drawn across the entrance and a fire of timbers burning in a hearth below a flue through the roof. A hammock stretched between two masts in the flickering firelight and, inside it, a body stirred. Bryony froze, the clippers for cutting a locket chain poised in her hand. Suddenly a voice squawked from the shadows: "Keep yer thieving fingers off my gold."

A large parrot flapped from its perch and dive-bombed her as she crouched behind a barrel, just escaping an aerial, as well as a verbal attack. In all the kerfuffle, the hammock swung and an angry grunt emerged from it. "What's goin' on? Shut the row, Hornswaggle, or I'll pluck yer like a chicken and roast yer on a spit."

The parrot circled the cave before returning to its perch with a grumpy-sounding, "Shiver Me Timbers".

PIRATE STORIES

Still stooping out of sight while a flutter of feathers settled, Bryony waited for the sound of heavy breathing from the hammock, with its half-empty bottle of rum beneath it. Soon snores and splutters convinced her to creep over, despite threatening squawks from the parrot.

In the glow from the fire, Bryony saw the sleeping face, weathered and wizened, with salt-encrusted wrinkles and wind-blasted whiskers. Under the scraggly white beard, she glimpsed a fine chain around the pirate's neck, so she slowly raised the clippers and edged them towards his throat. She stretched out her other hand to lift the locket very gently to slide the blades around it. Like a surgeon performing a delicate operation, she snipped through the chain, swiftly pulled the locket free and nimbly slipped outside.

As the sun began to rise over the sea and the first light of dawn shone on two scraps of parchment in Breon's lap, he tried to make sense of the puzzle. He placed them side by side but they were more confusing than ever: 6S9 MN and BS NEWS 5/10/20.

Bryony couldn't make sense of them, either. "Maybe the numbers are a date. Could it be 5th October 1720? And what can BS or NEWS mean? It's hopeless. We've come all this way and we're going to let Grandpa down after all."

Bones sighed. "Don't ask me to work it out. It don't make no sense to me, either."

Suddenly a hand snatched both scraps from Breon's hands as pistols rattled and pointed at each of them. A shrill squeal came from a woman who looked like an enormous raven. She had a baggy black cape that flapped like wings, a hooked beak-like nose, a black feathered bycoket hat and the scariest orange eyes with centres like smouldering lead shot. Her manic stare was full of anger, hate and madness. "Just what I've been looking for," she squawked. "I bet O'Malley sent you. Get ready to die."

Birdie Raven looked far more frightening than they'd feared. She was pointing a pistol directly at Breon's head, while two evil-looking henchmen stood beside her, each aiming muskets with their fingers twitching on the triggers.

"The Dead Man's Chest will be mine at last – while you'll all be strung up for the ants to bite you to bits before the vultures rip you to shreds. Tie them up – I want their deaths to be slow so I can delight in their screams. Take them to the Blood Stone while I crack this code."

"That's it! Blood Stone!" Breon exclaimed. "That's what BS must mean on the puzzle. I think I know what the rest means, too. In fact, we could help you crack the code so you can find the treasure. It might be worth keeping us alive, after all!"

The look in her eyes changed from fury to utter irritation, as she realised Breon could be right. Even though he was bluffing and had no idea what the rest of the puzzle meant, he knew it was worth playing for time. She snapped her fingers and one of her pirates frisked them and took away their knives.

"You'll still be tied to the Blood Stone. As soon as I've found the treasure, you'll be smeared with honey and left to the ants, vultures and maggots. Flies will lay eggs in your flesh and as you die, you'll be wriggling with insect life. That always attracts ravenous pecking birds."

She even laughed like a cawing raven.

The sun beat down on the Blood Stone, a pillar of ancient rock jutting up from a slope of volcanic ash and scrub. Wisps of smoke rose from a crater at the top of the slope and the smoky mist smelt of rotten eggs... and the remains of the last victims. Firmly tied with their backs to the stone, Breon, Bryony and Bones faced the strutting Birdie, the bad-tempered Skullery (who appeared with a parrot on his shoulder), and the two sneering henchmen with spades.

"I say we kill 'em all now," Skullery began. "I reckon I can work out this puzzle without them. Just before I killed Iron-Fist Frank, he told me the letters were directions of the compass and the numbers were paces. So, you see, I don't need your help."

"I told you what BS means, but what about NEWS?" Breon wasn't giving up. "And you'll certainly need my help when you get to the last bit." He was still bluffing.

"If you try any nonsense, you'll regret it," Birdie screeched. "At your feet is a pit full of the deadliest snakes on earth and by midday, this slope will be alive with boa constrictors sunning themselves and looking for prey. They devoured our last intruders and I could still hear them screaming from inside the snakes as they were slowly being digested."

Suddenly Skullery shouted, sending the parrot squawking above his head. "I don't know what NEWS means in that puzzle. The numbers mean five paces one way, then ten, then twenty in another direction – but what is NEWS?"

"Oh, that's easy," Bryony said, with a flash of inspiration. "NE is North East, W is West and S is South."

"Blimey, she's right!" Skullery barked, as he took out his compass, took five paces north-east from the Blood Stone (carefully avoiding the snake pit), then turned west, took ten paces, then turned south and paced twenty steps.

"Here," he shouted to his men, "Get digging!"

The dust blew across the hillside as their spades clattered through the earth and ash.

Eventually one of the men stopped, bent down and pulled a large brass key from the hole.

"That's it! That's the key to the Dead Man's Chest. Now we've got to find the chest. My piece of paper tells me where it is from here." Both Skullery and Birdie studied the letters and numbers, as their henchmen filled in the hole.

Bones whispered to his friends tied with him, "Don't move, but I'm about to cut us all free while they're not looking. Keep holding the ropes so it looks like we're still tied up."

His blade flashed so fast, he'd sliced through the ropes in seconds. "Easier than filleting a flounder with a flick-knife," he smiled.

"Wherever were you hiding that blade?" Breon was stunned.

"My little secret."

Bryony looked up at the sky directly above them. Already the vultures were circling.

"It must be six paces north, then nine... what

does MN mean?" Skullery was almost pulling his beard out with rage. He pointed a pistol directly at Bones. "I hate puzzles. Tell me what MN means or you're dead."

"That's simple," Bones chuckled. "It stands for Mid Night. If you all turn around and look out over the sea, it will become clear from the stars out there tonight." He was bluffing so convincingly that they all turned to look out to sea. As soon as they all had their backs to the Blood Stone, Bones whispered instructions to his friends. Within seconds, they were running down the hill, whirring ropes in the air and knocking their captors to the ground, catching each of them completely off guard. Grabbing pistols, spades and daggers, Breon and Bryony could only laugh at the ranting from Birdie, the raging from Skullery and the swearing from the parrot. The two burly henchmen charged at Bones before he had the chance to raise a weapon.

They hurled themselves at him but his nifty footwork, ducking punches and quick shoulder throws sent both men sprawling... straight into the snake pit. Their screams were silenced when the first fangs struck.

"I'll never let you get your hands on the treasure," Birdie shouted, tearing up the parchment. "If I can't have it, no one will." She ripped it into tiny pieces and threw them into the wind.

Breon put his head in his hands. "We'll never find it now. Grandpa will be devastated."

Bryony sat in deep thought while Bones pointed pistols and said, "I can see why you're called Birdie Raven. You're stark RAVEN mad!"

She snapped, "I wish I'd strung you upside down by your toenails when I had the chance."

"Upside down!" Bryony snapped. "That's it! They had it upside down. It wasn't 6 S 9 M N at all. The other way up is N W 6 S 9. That's

north-west six paces, followed by nine to the
south."

Breon was already pacing from where they'd
dug up the key. "North-west, six paces. South,
nine paces. It's under here. Dead Man's Chest is
right here."

He and Bones began digging, while Bryony
wound ropes around the two pirates, now
shouting uncontrollably. They almost exploded
when the spades hit something solid and, after a
lot of scraping, when a large chest was carefully
lifted from the hole. With a turn of the key, a
creaking open of the lid and a flash of the most
glorious treasure, Bryony and Breon danced,
while Bones cheered and sang. Had their hands
not been firmly tied, the screaming pirates would
have throttled one another in their blistering,
spitting rage – each blaming the other for their
furious misery.

Rowing away from Sabretooth Island with the

Dead Man's Chest glinting in the sunlit boat, Bones pulled on the oars with a beaming smile. "Your grandpa will be over the moon."

"I can't wait to tell him and see his face when we show him the treasure," Bryony grinned.

"I wonder what Skullery will do now," she pondered.

"He won't last long," Bones said. "I had to leave them tied up so they wouldn't fire their cannons at us as we head off. They were last seen wrestling with an enormous hungry boa constrictor so even if they survive that, they'll probably tear each other to shreds or vultures will finish them both off."

"It looks like they're already swooping," said Breon, pointing to huge birds circling over the island. "I suppose it's a fitting way for Birdie to meet her end with a name like hers. I think there must be something about pirates and birds."

Bones chuckled, "Did you know Birdie Raven

has a pirate brother? He's Jack Sparrow!"

As they giggled, two parrots landed in the boat, squawking "Dead Man's Chest, Dead Man's Chest, Dead Man's Chest."

"It looks like they want to come with us," Bryony said, as one hopped onto her arm.

"If I'm not mistaken," Breon added thoughtfully, "that is a Cuban Macaw and the other is a Jamaican Parakeet, and they've just given me an idea for the title of our story. How about Parrots of the Caribbean?"

"It sounds like an absolute winner," they laughed.

THE LIGHTHOUSE KEEPER'S SECRET

A slippery melodrama featuring:
Storyteller
Lighthouse Keeper (LK)
Iris (his daughter)
Mother (his wife)
Eye-Patch Jake —
an evil pirate (EPJ)

SHIVERS

The scene is a downstairs kitchen in a lighthouse. A flashing torch on a table will serve as the great lamp. Each time characters climb up or down the tower, they go round and round the lamp with heavy strides (clockwise for up and anti-clockwise for down).

Storyteller: This is a tale to chill your nerves, to make your blood run cold, to turn your knees to jelly and to freeze your heart to ice...

LK: Then I'd better throw a lump of coal on the fire.

Mother: And I'd better let the cat in.

Iris: But mother, this is a lighthouse perched on a rock with a roaring sea all around.

Mother: No wonder that cat always comes in

soaked to the skin.

Storyteller: This is a tale to send a shiver down your spine...

LK : Aaah. A shiver just shot down my spine. It went down my trouser leg and into the cat's saucer of milk. Look, it's now frozen solid.

Mother: The milk?

LK: No, the cat.

Iris: Oooh, mother – just hark at that wind and sea.

Storyteller: Whoooosh... shshshshshs...

Mother: It's a dark and stormy evening, alright.

SHIVERS

Storyteller: It was a dark and stormy evening.

LK: You can say that again.

Storyteller: I just did. The wind howled at the one solid iron door. Whoooooooooosh!

LK: Just hark at the wind howling at the one solid iron door.

Storyteller: The huge waves lashed up at every window. Lash... splash... splosh.

Mother: Just hark at those huge waves lashing up at every window.

Storyteller: The spray froze into icicles on the lighthouse walls.

LK : Just hark at the spray freezing into icicles on the lighthouse walls.

Iris: But father, icicles don't make a noise.

LK : So that's why it's gone deathly quiet. But look at the time – it's almost nightfall.

Storyteller: Bang... crash... wallop!

Iris: Eek, what was that?

LK : Night. It just fell. But now I must get to work – to climb those steps and light the lamp to save the poor sailors on this dark and stormy night. I pity any ship out there. At least our lamp will save them from the rocks. So up I shall go, taking a candle with me...*(He begins walking round and round)* Up and up and up. Round and round and round.

SHIVERS

Storyteller: So up he went: up and up and up. Round and round and round. Up and round, up and round, up and round, and up some more...

LK: Round and up, round and up, round and up.

Storyteller: Upward, climbing ever upward...

LK: Up and...

Storyteller: Round, round and...

LK: Up some more...

Storyteller: Round and up, round and up, up and round, up and round... until...

LK : I've reached the top!

Storyteller: The great lamp stood in front of him.

LK : The great lamp stands in front of me. Its wick will be a beacon for all.

Storyteller: He put the flame to the wick. A flicker... then a flash. It's alight!

LK : Well that's another day's work done. Now the beam will light the ocean. Over the angry sea...

Storyteller: Through the howling storm...

LK : Before I go back down, there is one thing I must do.

SHIVERS

Storyteller: His icy hand fumbled in his icy pocket.

LK: The key... the key... where is the key?

Storyteller: His icy hand kept fumbling... and fumbling. Every place a key might be.

LK: Aha – here it is.

Storyteller: He crept into the shadows where a large sea-chest was locked and bolted.

LK: The rusty lock must yield... *(coughs)* I've always had trouble with my chest.

Storyteller: With that, he slowly lifted the heavy, dusty lid.

LK: Each night I make sure this is safe.

PIRATE STORIES

Storyteller: And with that, his icy hand shook as he slowly took from the chest a small golden box and gently... ever so gently... opened the lid.

LK: Ah, my little beauty – still mine. One day you'll repay me in my old age.

Storyteller: As he stroked the box before returning it inside the chest, his wife and daughter downstairs heated the supper on the stove just as heavy drumming came from the iron door.

Iris: Eek – what is it?

Mother: It's heavy drumming coming from the iron door.

Iris: On a night like this?

SHIVERS

Mother: Then it can mean only one thing.

Iris: Oh mother – tell me what. What can it mean, mother? Oh mother, what?

Mother: Someone wants to come in.

Storyteller: And with that, the great iron door flew open and there – against the roaring gale and lit only by a flash of lightning, stood…

Eye-**P**atch **J**ake: Me!

Mother: Who?

EPJ: I.

Iris: I?

Mother: I?

EPJ: No, only one eye... I've got one missing! I'm Eye-Patch Jake and you're doomed.

Mother: Please, no – not Eye-Patch Jake!

Iris: Not here in our kitchen?

Mother: Not Jake – with the eye-patch and slimy scar down his left cheek?

Iris: The pirate with blood on his hands and a price on his head!

Mother: Known as 'The Butcher of the Seas'?

EPJ: So you've heard of me?

Mother: No.

Storyteller: With lips like lard, his greasy

smile glistened in the candlelight.

E P J: I've come to seek my revenge. Where's the Lighthouse Keeper?

Storyteller: He pulled a rope from his coat and tied them both up. Round and round.

E P J: Round and round and round.

Iris: Something fishy is going on here.

E P J: It's my rope – sorry about the smell. Now to climb the steps and plunge my cutlass into the Lighthouse Keeper's back and get my revenge before I blow this place sky high.

Mother: Oh no – you mean....

E P J: Yes, I've got enough gunpowder in my

pockets to sink a ship. Ha ha ha.

Iris: No, please! No, please! No, please!

Storyteller: He began to creep up the twisting lighthouse steps...

EPJ: Round and up, round and up, round and up...

Storyteller: Up and round, up and round, up and round...

EPJ: Higher and higher...

Storyteller: Faster and faster...

EPJ: Round and up, round and up, round and up...

Storyteller: Up and round, up and round, up

and round... until at last he reached...

EPJ: The top!

Storyteller: The Lighthouse Keeper had just closed the chest.

LK: Who's there?

EPJ: Me.

LK: Eh?

EPJ: Eye...

LK: Where?

EPJ: Patch...

LK: What?

EPJ: Jake.

LK: Who?

EPJ: Jake.

LK: Jake? Not... Eye-Patch Jake with one eye?

EPJ: Got it. I'm the pirate with one eye, called Jake.

LK: Oh really? So what's your other eye called?

EPJ: And I spy with that little eye something beginning with REVENGE.

LK: I'll never tell my secret. My lips are sealed. You'll never make me talk.

EPJ: I've got a razor-sharp cutlass for slicing your gizzard.

LK: What do you want to know? *(He drops to the ground, whimpering)*

Storyteller: The Lighthouse Keeper lost his cool.

EPJ: What are you doing down there?

LK: It's my cool – I've lost it. I'll find it in a minute.

EPJ: Bah! You know what I want.

LK: Yes, I know.

EPJ: And I know, too.

LK : I know you know.

EPJ : And I know you know I know.

LK : I know.

Storyteller : He knew.

EPJ : I know too.

Storyteller : He knew too.

EPJ : I've been hunting for you for years – keeping an eye out for you.

LK : So that's why it's missing.

Storyteller : The Lighthouse Keeper suddenly swung round the great lamp to flash right into Jake's one eye.

SHIVERS

EPJ: Aaaaaaagh!

Storyteller: The cutlass fell from the pirate's hand and they pulled and punched, pushed and gripped. They began to tumble... down the lighthouse steps... round and round and round, down and down and down – until the Lighthouse Keeper cracked his head and slumped with a groan.

EPJ: Ah ha! Knocked out. Now to search his pockets for what I'm after...

Storyteller: Meanwhile, down in the kitchen, the rope was working loose...

Mother: At last, this rope smells of fish.

Storyteller: The cat chewed through the last fishy threads.

PIRATE STORIES

Iris: We're free! Quick, we must rush to father's rescue...

Storyteller: They grabbed a candle and a rolling pin and began the long climb, just as Eye-Patch Jake dragged the Lighthouse Keeper back upstairs.

EPJ: Up and up and round and round...

Storyteller: Round and round and up and up...

Mother: Up and round and round and up...

Iris: Round and round and up and up...

EPJ: Higher, ever higher...

Storyteller: Step after step after step...

SHIVERS

Mother: One after another after another...

Iris: Upwards, ever upwards...

EPJ: I've reached the top!

Storyteller: Fumbling in the flashing darkness, Eye-Patch Jake caught sight of his glinting cutlass – while the two women climbed on and on...

Mother: Round and round and up and up...

EPJ: Ah ha ha... time to cut his throat...

Iris: We've reached the top!

Storyteller: Before Eye-Patch Jake could grab the cutlass, the Lighthouse Keeper's wife coshed him with her rolling pin and he slithered to the floor in a trickle of slime.

M other: We'll lock him in that chest – the key is still in it. Then we'll drag it up onto the roof and keep him out the way till the navy arrives. They'll take him away to prison and we'll all be safe evermore.

Iris: But he might freeze to death up there on a night like this.

M other: I'll throw a candle in with him to keep him warm. *(Does so)*

Storyteller: So, they shoved him in the chest and took out the little golden box.

M other: I can't think what this is. More junk to throw away. *(Drops it on the floor)*

SHIVERS

Storyteller: With that, they dragged the chest up the steps to the roof...

Iris: Push... up and round....

Mother: Pull... round and up...

Storyteller: Puffing and panting, step by step, they came to the hatch that led out onto the roof, high above the angry rocks below....

Iris: The wind is so strong and cold and terrifying.

Storyteller: Just as a gust ripped through the night sky, they slammed the hatch behind them.

Mother: The chest must take its chance up there. Now down we go...

PIRATE STORIES

Iris: Down and round and down...

Mother: We'll have to get your father down to the kitchen...

Storyteller: So they dragged him down and round and round and down...

Iris: Round and down...

Mother: Down and round...

Storyteller: Down and down and down; round and round and round.

Iris: Down and round, down and round, down and round.

Mother: At last, we've reached the ground.

SHIVERS

Storyteller: They put the Lighthouse Keeper in a chair by the fire. *(They sit.)* But there was no time to lose. *(They stand.)*

Mother: My dear, your father's too ill, I am too old and there's an evil pirate up there on the roof in a chest. He might break out and murder us all and take this bag – our life savings. You must escape with it and row to shore right now.

Iris: But mother, I'll never be able to spend it tonight!

Mother: No, my child. Just take the little boat tied up outside and get away fast.

Iris: But the sea is so wild, the waves are so high, the wind is so strong, the air is so cold, the storm is so fierce, the night is so dark, the gale is so rough, the land is so far...

Mother: Then you'd better take my umbrella. You must be brave, Iris.

Storyteller: Iris took the bag of money and they wept – even the cat shed a tear. As the door opened, the howling storm took their breath away.

Mother: Row to land. Put the money in the bank and go to Uncle Ronald's. Get a big pack of guys and some navy ships.

Storyteller: Whoooosh, crassssh, rumble, hooouooooowl.

Iris: I can't hear you, mother, but I'll do my best....

Storyteller: While the storm raged on, the poor girl squatted in the boat with a barnacled bottom (the boat, not the girl). Mother shut the great iron door, just as a wave washed away the bag of money from the girl's hand and she was whisked away into the cruel night. Suddenly, a flash lit up the sky, like a rocket shooting from the top of the lighthouse.

M other: Hark, upstairs – was that lightning striking the roof? I must pop up to see.

Storyteller: She began to climb in the dark and cold. Up and up....

M other: Up and up and round and round ....

Storyteller: Higher and higher, round and up, round and up, round and up...

M other: Puffing, panting, swirling, twirling, dizzy, giddy...

Storyteller: Past the great flashing lamp and up the last few steps – to peep outside.

Mother: Oh no, it's gone!

Storyteller: All that was left on the scorched roof was a trickle of slime. The gunpowder inside Eye-Patch Jake's pocket had ignited from the candle and he'd been blown to smithereens.

Mother: It serves him right.

Storyteller: With that, she began the downward plod – down and round...

Mother: Bit by bit, step by step, round and down like a corkscrew...

Storyteller: Down and round, down and round, until at last she reached...

SHIVERS

Mother: The ground! My dear, you're stirring. That pirate's gone – with the chest.

LK: The chest? Not my special chest. No, I must go up and see for myself...

Storyteller: Feeble as he was, he staggered up the twisting steps. Up and round...

LK: Upward, ever upward. Round and ever roundward....

Storyteller: Up in the darkness, lit every few seconds by the blinding flash, something caught his eye.

LK: Aha, there's my golden box, my little beauty. Oh no, is it empty?

Storyteller: With shaking fingers, he slowly

opened the lid. Peeping up at him on a cushion of black velvet... stared an eye.

LK : Ha ha! Eye-Patch Jake won't want you again so you're mine forever!

Storyteller: The red eye winked, as the Lighthouse Keeper turned to go down...

LK : Down and round, down and round, down and round...

Storyteller: Down and round, down and round, until, at last, he reached the ground.

Mother: Why are you grinning, husband? What have you got in that box? Eeeek! What do you want with that horrid bloodshot eye?

LK : It's a long story but at last I must tell you.

SHIVERS

Long ago, long before we met, I'm ashamed to say I was a pirate. I was in Eye-Patch Jake's gang when he had two eyes – as he wore this false one. When I told him I'd had enough of being a pirate, we fought – oh, how we fought – and his false eye popped out when I smashed a barrel over his head.

M o t h e r: Typical pirates.

LK : After I escaped and took off my shirt, I found the false eye – it had lodged in my belly button. It's a ruby, worth a fortune. I knew he would never rest till he tracked me down to get it back and seek revenge. But now he's gone, this eye will see us into our old age! We'll never have to worry about money again. So why are you crying, my dear?

M o t h e r: It's our daughter. I shall never rest

until Iris returns. Why ever did I send her out on such a cruel night as this?

LK: But haven't you noticed? It is morning and all is calm. The storm is over.

Storyteller: As a golden sun rose above the quiet sea, a small rowing boat drifted up to the rocks. Iris climbed the steps up to the great iron door.

Mother: It's Iris – oh my daughter!

Iris: Mother... father... *(all three embrace)*

Storyteller: They all hugged – while the cat shed another tear.

Mother: But Iris, where's the navy? I sent you to fetch them.

SHIVERS

Iris: Did you? I thought you wanted these. Look inside the bag.

Mother: I said 'go to Uncle Ronald's to get a big pack of guys and some navy ships.'

Iris: Ooh. I didn't hear you in that wind. I thought you said "Go to McDonald's and get A BIG MAC and FRIES and SOME GRAVY CHIPS". Oops!

Mother: Well at least our life's savings are safe, aren't they?

Iris: Oh mother, please forgive me. They're at the bottom of the sea. I'm so sorry! We are ruined. Ruined, do you hear – RUINED!

Mother: Think nothing of it, love. We'll turn a blind eye. This one. Worth a fortune.

PIRATE STORIES

Iris: But Mother, Father, I don't understand. How can it be?

LK: It's a long story but it goes like this, my girl. Long ago before you were born, Iris, I was on a pirate ship at sea. It was a dark and stormy night...

(The actors freeze. The Storyteller walks to the front of the stage.)

Storyteller: Our tale is told, it must be said,
And One-Eyed Jake is finally dead.
The ending of our tale is told...
The Lighthouse Keeper had his gold.
That ruby eye fetched such a price,
A fortune that was rather nice!
They moved away and joy was theirs...
No more they trod those wretched stairs.
Their ups and downs had gone – and so

SHIVERS

They bought a cosy bungalow.

Our play is done, but don't get stroppy...

You can always buy a PIRATE copy!

PIRATE STORIES

SHIVERS

PIRATEY FACTS

Did you know....

1. Piracy is the act of boarding a ship with intent to use force to commit theft or any other crime. This has probably existed ever since the first boats set sail, but the first recorded description comes from Egyptian records of the 14th century BCE, when Lukkan pirates from Turkey's Mediterranean coast raided boats at Cyprus.

2. Although the origin of the name "Jolly Roger" for the skull and crossbones flag on top of a pirate ship is unknown, one theory comes from the use of red flags. Long ago, a red flag was sometimes used during naval warfare to show that no mercy would be given to anyone captured (they would be killed immediately).

PIRATE STORIES

Called a Joli Rouge ('pretty red') by the French,
this may have been translated into English
as Jolly Roger. Another theory suggests Jolly
Roger came from 'Old Roger', a term for the
Devil.

3. Not all pirate ships flew a Jolly Roger
flag. Many pirates had their own designs, such
as Blackbeard, whose own black flag showed
a skeleton with horns. The skeleton held an
hourglass in one hand, and in the other he
carried a spear pointing to a heart dripping
with three drops of blood (pages 51 and 54).

4. Being a pirate wasn't just for men. Lady
Killigrew (page 83) was far from the only
female associated with piracy. Other famous
women pirates were Mary Read, Anne Bonny,
Grace O' Malley and Ching Shih (all very scary
and bloodthirsty).

5. The pirate's drink of choice was called grog – a mixture of rum, water, lemon juice and sugar. Mind you, they'd probably swig anything going!

6. Some pirates really did wear eye patches. Apparently, one reason could have been to keep one eye 'in the dark' so it adjusted better to night vision and seeing below deck in the gloom. Don't try it. In fact, another strange rumour has it that pirates wore earrings because they thought ear-piercing improved their eyesight!

7. Pirates didn't really go in for forcing people to walk the plank. Most pirates just killed people straight away. When they did torture their prisoners, it was usually through keelhauling (dragging a tied sailor in the water from the back of the ship), marooning a person on a deserted island or lashing them with a leather whip.

GLOSSARY

apothecary an old-fashioned word for someone who prepared and sold medicines.

cutlass a short sword with a gently curved blade, often used by sailors in the past.

flotsam cargo from a ship that has been washed overboard and found floating at sea or on the shore.

highwayman someone who robbed travellers using a weapon and then escaped on horseback.

quay a platform sticking out into the water from which the passengers and cargo on a ship can be loaded or unloaded.